Manufactured in the United States of America   3 4 5 6 7 8 9 0   A B C D E F G H I J K

Book Club Edition

Walt Disney Productions
presents

A WHITE CHRISTMAS

Random House 🏠 New York

It was two days before Christmas.

Donald Duck's nephews were staring out their bedroom window.

"Look at that awful rain," said Huey.

"We won't have any snow for Christmas," said Dewey.

"And that means no skiing, no sledding, and no skating," said Louie.

Louie found a picture of a skier.

"Look at what we're missing," he said.

"You know," said Huey, "there is always snow in the mountains."

"Let's ask Uncle Donald to take us to the mountains for Christmas!" said Louie.

The boys ran downstairs.
Donald was busy trimming
the Christmas tree.

"Uncle Donald," said the boys,
"let's go away to the mountains
so we can have a white Christmas."

"Go away?" said Donald. "But
we are all ready for Christmas
at home. I just have to finish
trimming the tree."

The doorbell rang.

"That must be Daisy," said Donald.

"Go and let her in, boys."

"Hi, Daisy," said the boys. "We just had
a great idea. Let's go to the mountains for
a white Christmas."

"Sounds like fun," said Daisy.

"It's the craziest thing I ever heard of," said Donald. "We are all ready for Christmas at home."

"You can always change your plans," said Daisy. "Let the boys run down to the travel agency. See what they can find out."

"Oh, all right," said Donald.

"Off you go, boys," said Daisy.
"I'll bake some cookies for you while
you are gone."

"Gee, thanks," said the boys.

"And bundle up," added Daisy.
"It's getting colder."

Huey, Dewey, and Louie set off
in the chilling rain.

Over at Mickey's house, no one liked
the rain either.

Mickey had had a bad cold all week.
The rain made him feel worse.

"Here, have some hot tea," said Minnie.
"It will make you feel better."

"Wouldn't it be nice to go somewhere
warm for Christmas?" asked Minnie.
"Think of sitting on a beach . . ."

". . . with warm sun and soft breezes," said Mickey. "Great!"

"I'll run down to the travel agency and find out where we could go," said Minnie.

She put on her coat.

It was very
nasty outside.
Minnie was
chilled to the
bone.

Minnie ran into Donald's nephews.

"Where are you going in this awful weather?"
she asked.

"To the travel agency," said the boys.

"So am I!" said Minnie.

Minnie and the boys walked on together.

Inside the travel agency they saw
wonderful posters.

"Oh, look at that sun!" said Minnie.

"Oh, look at that snow!" said the boys.

Along came Uncle Scrooge McDuck.
He saw the group in the travel agency.
"Hmmm, I wonder what they are up to,"
said Scrooge. "I think I'll go inside."

Minnie and the
boys told Scrooge
all about their
travel plans for
Christmas.

"A waste of money!" said
Scrooge. "Who cares about
Christmas anyway?"
"We do!" yelled the boys.

"Bah, humbug!" said Scrooge as
they all left the travel agency.

Minnie invited the boys back to
Mickey's house for a cup of cocoa.
They found Mickey eating soup
in front of the fire.
He was feeling a little better.

"Look at these travel pictures!"
said the boys.

"I can see us now," said Minnie, "putting
on our sunglasses . . ."

". . . putting on our skis," said the boys.

While the boys drank their cocoa, they
saw a wonderful sight!

"The rain has turned to snow!"
cried Dewey.

"It's sticking to the ground!"
said Huey.

"It's getting deeper by the minute!"
said Louie.

The boys put on their coats
and ran out to play in the snow.

People were already skiing
and sledding.

"Wheee!" cried the boys as
they slid down a hill.

Back home Donald
and Daisy were getting
worried.

"Where could those
kids be?" wondered
Donald.

"Maybe the boys stopped off
to visit Goofy," said Daisy.
"I'll give him a call."

And she went to the phone.

Goofy was getting
dressed to go out
when the phone rang.

"Hello? ...
Oh, hi, Daisy. ...
No, I haven't seen
the boys. But I'll
go out and look
for them."

"Yes, I'll
tell them to
hurry home."

"You're welcome.
Good-bye."

Goofy soon found the boys.

"How about a ride on my sled?" asked Goofy.
He forgot all about Daisy's phone call.

Then Goofy had a snowball fight with
the boys.

Finally Goofy remembered the time.

"Uncle Donald will be mad at us
for being so late," said Huey. "Please
come home with us, Goofy, and
help us explain!"

So Goofy picked up his sled and
went home with the boys.

Donald was not angry after all.
He was just happy to see the boys.
"Come on in and look at the tree,"
said Daisy.

"Wow, that's the most beautiful tree I ever saw!" said Goofy. "You folks sure are lucky to be spending Christmas at home."

The boys quietly dumped their travel pictures.

Daisy served hot cider and
her freshly baked cookies.

"You know, Goofy," she said,
"we WERE thinking of going to
the mountains for Christmas."

"We changed our minds," said the boys.
"We can have our white Christmas here
at home."

"Come spend Christmas with us, Goofy," said Donald.

"I'd love to," said Goofy. "But I just promised to go away with Mickey and Minnie!"

"Let me talk to Minnie," said Daisy.

She picked up the phone.

Minnie and Mickey were busy choosing
things to take on their trip.

Minnie stopped to look out the window.
"How pretty the snow is!" she said.

"It's almost a shame
to leave," said Mickey.

Just then the phone rang.
Minnie answered it.

She began to smile.

"Mickey," she called. "It's
Daisy. She wants us to spend
an old-fashioned white Christmas
with them! What do you say?"

"Yes, let's!" said Mickey.
"Christmas is a time to be
with friends. And my cold
is getting better."

And so it was settled.

Everyone would spend Christmas together at home.

On Christmas Day, Mickey and Minnie picked up Grandma Duck in Mickey's car.

"Let's go and get Scrooge too," said Grandma.

Scrooge was still in his dressing gown.

"We stayed home after all," said Mickey.
"Come with us to the Christmas party at
Donald's place."

"Bah, humbug," said Scrooge.

But he got dressed anyway and came
along.

Everyone had a good time at Donald's house—even Scrooge.

"A toast!" said Donald.

He lifted his cup of eggnog.

"Here's to our beautiful, merry white Christmas at home!" he said.

"Hooray!" cried Huey, Dewey, and Louie.

Then they all went skating.

What a wonderful Christmas it was!